Erasmus Among the Luminaries

"I love logic, the beauty and poetry of it, and that was one of the main reasons I enjoyed *Erasmus Among the Luminaries*. There's a lightness to it because of the back and forth of the dialogue. Such big ideas carried along so lightly. Such deep ideas all hovering on the surface where they become entertaining. It could so easily have been something going off in all directions. The focus on the body in the middle was a stroke of genius in terms of staging. And all the time levels are deftly interwoven. A brilliant work of art."

—Magdalene Redekop, author of *Making Believe*

"A brilliant cross-examination of a cross-section of Luminaries who throw light and shade while playfully taking time out for tea."

—David E. Ortman, Attorney-at-Law

"If Socrates, Hrosvitha, Aquinas, and Gandhi are among your fantasy tea party guests, pull up a chair for *Erasmus Among the Luminaries*! Envisioning the afterlife as a sparkling debate among history's great thinkers, Friesen invites us to ponder big questions of faith, goodness, and beauty with both depth and cheek."

—Melissa Friesen, Mary Nord and Joseph Ignat Endowed Chair in Theatre, Bluffton University

"Lauren Friesen mines a rich seam of intellectual history to deliver this gem of a conversation among world intellects, who gather in 'A Room in the Great Beyond' in hopes that the newly-arrived Dutch humanist Erasmus (1466–1535) can settle a controversy among them: 'What is good?' One part *Waiting for Godot*, one part *No Exit*, three parts philosophical fantasia, Friesen's *Erasmus* should be required reading for every university survey of comparative thought in religion—which is how I'll be employing it in the one I teach."

—Lee Krähenbühl, Professor of Communication, Stevenson University

Erasmus Among the Luminaries
A Fantasy in Two Parts

Lauren D. Friesen

FOREWORD BY
Eric MacPhail

RESOURCE *Publications* · Eugene, Oregon

ERASMUS AMONG THE LUMINARIES
A Fantasy in Two Parts

Resource Publications
An Imprint of Wipf and Stock Publishers
199 W. 8th Ave., Suite 3
Eugene, OR 97401

www.wipfandstock.com

PAPERBACK ISBN: 979-8-3852-6817-7
HARDCOVER ISBN: 979-8-3852-6818-4
EBOOK ISBN: 979-8-3852-6819-1

VERSION NUMBER 12/15/25

lfriesen@umich.edu
    or
Friesenjl1970@gmail.com

Cover:
Line drawing by Janet Friesen
Mask photo: Lauren Friesen

Contents

Foreword

Eric MacPhail

Indiana University

Editor, *Erasmus Studies*

Desiderius Erasmus was the foremost humanist of the Northern European Renaissance. He was born in Rotterdam, probably in 1469, and he died in Basel, Switzerland, in 1536. In between, he led an eventful and productive life that brought him into contact and conflict with nearly all the important political, religious, and literary figures of his time. He was a prolific author of works in all possible genres, except for the theater, but he did write a number of dialogues, known as the *Colloquies*, that were used for pedagogical purposes to teach young students Latin and may well have been performed as school plays. He also edited the comedies of the ancient Roman playwright Terence. He is best remembered as a letter writer and a controversialist, and for his edition of the New Testament, including the first printed Greek text, a revised Latin translation, and an extensive set of annotations. Erasmus is variously understood as rhetorician, a religious thinker, a philosopher, a pedagogue, a satirist, an epistolographer, a courtier, a political thinker, and an indefatigable compiler of ancient wit and wisdom. He inspired a tradition of religious tolerance and reconciliation known as Erasmianism, and his legacy lives on today in the European university fellowship program named after him. He is, as a recent monograph puts it, a man without frontiers.[1]

---

1. Lucia Felici, *Senza frontiere: L'Europa di Erasmo (1538–1600)* (Rome: Carocci, 2021).

Since Erasmus spent his life in correspondence with his contemporaries, it is only fitting that he should spend his afterlife in dialogue with posterity. Already, in the seventeenth century, Fontenelle had the bright idea of pairing Erasmus with his former boss, the Holy Roman Emperor Charles V, in one of his *Dialogues of the Dead*. This literary tradition of dialogues of the dead goes back to the ancient Greek satirist Lucian of Samosata, some of whose works Erasmus translated from Greek into Latin with his friend Thomas More. So Erasmus gave an important impetus to this proto-theatrical genre. In the eighteenth century, Voltaire staged a dialogue between Lucian, Erasmus, and Rabelais in the Elysian Fields, which ends with the three of them joining Dean Swift, author of *Gulliver's Travels*, for lunch. Voltaire's version suggests that this conceit of the dialogue of authors is a kind of exercise in comparative literature, voicing the affinities and disparities between similar writers. Each such exercise constitutes a new literary corpus, almost like a bibliography.

One reason why it is so tricky to report Erasmus's words and sayings is that they usually aren't his. For instance, in the *Praise of Folly*, Erasmus avoids responsibility for his harsh criticisms by assuming the mask of Moria or Folly. She tells her audience in conclusion, "If anything I've said seems rather impudent or garrulous, you must remember it's Folly and a woman who's been speaking."[2] Moreover, she follows up that disclaimer with a proverb, "Often a foolish man speaks a word in season." These are neither her words nor Erasmus's, since proverbial wisdom doesn't belong to anyone. The one work which occupied Erasmus throughout his life was his collection of adages, which numbered 4,151 at his death. Erasmus is famous for sayings such as *Festina lente* or *Amicorum communia omnia*, which are not his but represent the collective wisdom of ages. At the same time, Erasmus is in complete agreement with Socrates, who is thought to have said to a prospective student, "Speak so that I can see you," since speech is the true mirror of the mind, even when we use someone else's words. Erasmus has

2. Erasmus, *Praise of Folly*, trans. Betty Radice, in *Collected Works of Erasmus*, ed. Ron Schoeffel et al., 89 vols. (Toronto: University of Toronto Press, 1974–), 27:153.

become so closely associated with proverbial sayings that Michel de Montaigne, in his *Essays*, remarks that if he could have seen Erasmus, he would have taken everything he said, including his instructions to his servants, as so many adages and apothegms. In effect, repeating the words of others has become the distinctive style of Erasmus; quotation is his way of speaking. This makes him a slippery spokesman for all the ideologies attributed to him, and it means that he continues to elude both his critics and his admirers in death as he did in life.

After such a dubious prologue, I would like to offer a sort of cento or tissue of quotations from Erasmus, drawn primarily from his correspondence, where he speaks in his own name. Erasmus is quick to remind his detractors that the author is distinct from the narrator of a literary text, and therefore you can't blame (or excommunicate) the author for what the narrator says. The narrative voice is fictional. We usually make an exception to this rule for letters, especially those not written for immediate publication and which might betray the unguarded thoughts of the author. Erasmus wrote nearly as many letters as adages, and they have all been translated into English for the *Collected Works of Erasmus* from the University of Toronto Press. In this edition, the letters are numbered 1 to 3141, including several written by his friends after his death. A number of these are referenced in the play.

Here goes:

> Ep. 1334: "The sum and substance of our religion is peace and concord."

> Ep. 182: "Compliments are nearly always harmful, while adverse criticism is always beneficial."

> Ep. 56: "Your first endeavour should be to choose the most learned teacher you can find, for it is impossible that one who is himself no scholar should make a scholar of anyone else."

> Ep. 1141: "I am filled with forebodings about that wretched Luther; the conspiracy against him is strong everywhere, and everywhere the ruling princes are against him, especially Pope Leo. If only he had followed my advice and refrained

from that offensive and seditious stuff! He would have done more good, and been much less unpopular. One man's undoing would be a small matter; but if they are successful in this campaign, their insolence will be past all bearing."

Ep. 480: "Pray consider the progress I have made: it is by writing so much that I have learnt to write badly."

Ep. 384: "Our chiefest hope for the restoration and rebuilding of the Christian religion, our sheet-anchor as they call it, is that all those who profess the Christian philosophy the whole world over should above all absorb the principles laid down they their Founder from the writings of the evangelists and apostles, in which that heavenly Word which once came down to us from the heart of the Father still lives and breathes for us and acts and speaks with more immediate efficacy, in my opinion, than in any other way."

Ep. 335: "Julius was a very great man—the fact that he embroiled almost the whole world in war shows that, I grant you; but to have restored peace to the world proves Leo greater still."

Ep. 337: "Nothing is so brazen, so pig-headed as ignorance. These are the men who conspire with such zeal against the humanities. Their aim is to count for something in the councils of the theologians, and they fear that if there is a renaissance of the humanities, and if the world sees the error of its ways, it may become clear that they know nothing, although in the old days they were commonly supposed to know everything."

Ep. 1581: "You suggest in your charity that my writings, unless amended, are dangerous to Christian faith: but I was equally convinced that it would be dangerous for the Christian faith if I held back the criticisms I wished to make."

Ep. 1549: "I have an adequate supply of Burgundy here."

Ep. 1524: "How I hate this ill health!—not so much for the torments I suffer from it, but it prevents my doing a kindness to any of my friends; so much harder is it to find oneself uncivil than unfortunate."

Ep. 1526: "What worries me now is that these common remedies, that is, recantations, imprisonment, and the stake, will simply make the evil worse. Two men were burned at Brussels, and it was precisely at that moment that the city began to support Luther."

Ep. 1690: "Those who foment sedition should be punished severely, but in such a way that the least possible harm is done to the innocent, that those who are capable of redemption are not driven away, and that the people are spared. Perhaps in those cities where the evil has taken root the best course will be to make room for both parties and to leave every man to his own conscience until the time comes when there is some hope of peace."

Ep. 2852: "But because I am caught between the knife and the altar [*inter sacrum et saxum*], as they say, since you will not let me make any excuse for not doing what you demand, and I on my part am unable to do it, I have found a middle course, by which I hope to render you more indulgent in the future."[3]

Erasmus lived his life in the shadow of religious controversy. He was a devout believer persecuted by clerics, monks, and theologians and harassed for lack of partisan spirit. He just wanted the world to get off his back, which is never a reasonable ambition. At least he didn't run out of Burgundy.

---

3. Quotes are from Erasmus, *Collected Works*, 9:245, 2:89, 1:113, 8:44, 4:102, 3:216, 3:99, 3:111, 11:135, 11:39, 10:448, 10:452, 12:141, 20:118.

Acknowledgments

A hearty thank you to Dale Schrag for his informative and inspiring class on Erasmus (2023).

The following read the early drafts and provided helpful feedback: Duane Friesen, Dale Schrag, Magdalene Redekop, Jeff and Cameron Altaras, Melissa Friesen, David Ortman, Arlo Kasper, and Daniel Born.

The Kennedy Center playwriting workshops and symposia created a network of supportive theater artists. The following need to be recognized for their tireless advocacy for new plays: Harlene Marley, Jeff Koep, Steve Sarratore, Marvin Sims, Kathryn Robinson, Ken Robbins, Jere Wade, Laurie Brooks, James Leonard Jr., Gary Garrison, Judith Royer, David Cohen, Tom Evans, Carolyn Gillespie, Sam Smiley, and Susan Shaffer.

Characters

Erasmus (1466–1535): Dutch humanist who resided in a monastery for eight years while in his youth. Prolific author who traveled and lectured across Northern Europe and England. His *Praise of Folly* appears in many anthologies.

Augustine of Hippo (354–430): Studied in Rome where he abandoned his hedonistic life. An African of Berber origin who became a monk and influenced Western Christianity with Neoplatonist views. His idealism continues to guide many today. Great art should be calm and devoid of emotional expressiveness.

Thomas Aquinas (?–1274): His books on theology began to provide significant alternatives to Augustine's idealistic view on religion and the arts. Aquinas valued human experience. Twelfth century. His empiricism was an alternative to Augustine's idealism.

Hillel of Babylon (c. 10 CE): Jewish religious leader, sage, and scholar associated with the development of the Mishnah and the Talmud and the founder of the House of Hillel. Often seen scribbling.

Hrostvitha of Gandersheim (Rose-vita, 935–973): Born into wealth and power, she became a canoness. The first known female playwright. Her best-known play is *Dulcitis* (*The Swain*).

Socrates (470–399 BCE): Greek philosopher. He showed how argument, debate, and discussion could help people understand complex issues. His probing way of teaching is called the "Socratic Method."

Hildegard von Bingen (1098–1179): The "Sibyl of the Rhine" was a German Benedictine abbess, mystic, and polymath active as a writer, composer, philosopher, mystic, and visionary who authored medical texts. At age ten she became an anchoress in a convent.

Immanuel Kant of Königsberg (1724–1804): German philosopher and one of the central thinkers of the Enlightenment. Art should be emotionally expressive and have a formal structure. The artist who can combine those two to create expressive form he identified as "genius." Devised the term *aesthetics*.

Mahatma K. Gandhi (1869–1948): Indian lawyer, anti-colonial nationalist, and political ethicist. Employed nonviolent resistance as a leader in the successful campaign for India's independence from British rule.

Susanne K. Langer (1895–1985): American philosopher. Developed the idea that rational thought arises from feelings. The first woman to be professionally recognized as a philosopher.

The American: A singer.

Time: Endless

Setting: A Room in the Great Beyond

Staged Reading
Kidron-Bethel Hall
North Newton, Kansas
September 16, 2025

Cast

American Singer—Carolyn Penner

Aquinas—Kent Little

Augustine—Rick Weaver

Erasmus—John McCabe-Juhnke

Gandhi—Chuck Regier

Hildegard von Bingen—Dorothy Nickel Friesen

Hillel—Doreen Esau

Hrostvitha—Marjean Harris

Immanuel Kant—Cliff Dick

Narrator—Darlene Dick

Socrates—Lauren Friesen

Susanne K. Langer—Jennifer Unruh

Production Assistants

Kathy Becker—Kidron Hall Logistics

Danny Keane—Technical Assistance

Monica Lichti—Prop Assistance

Keith and Judy Harder—Ushers

Part I

(Pre-show and post-show music: chants by Hildegard von Bingen. Such as the Voices of Angels album recording by the Voices of Ascension, conducted by Dennis Keene.)

Lights up on eight chairs, each with a small side table stacked with old books. The characters walk from table to table and now and then browse through a book. In the center is a simple cot with what appears to be a sleeping man under the covers. The chairs are occupied by Hillel the Elder, Thomas Aquinas, Augustine of Hippo, Hrostvitha of Gandersheim, Hildegard von Bingen, and Socrates. Three tables and chairs are without someone because Immanuel Kant, Mahatma Gandhi, and Susanne K. Langer arrive later. The characters often amble about browsing through books on the tables. Some browsers leave them on an empty chair or the floor. Hrostvitha walks from table to table to straighten the stacks because those who come to browse are afterwards rather sloppy in how they replace them. Now and then, there is distant thunder [a kettle drum] as the lights slowly rise. They also beat vigorously as the American Singer saunters in. Non-English spoken words are in italics.)

ERASMUS: *(Stirring in the cot, muttering.)* Hmmmm. Aaaaah.

AUGUSTINE: *(Soft voice.)* He's waking. *(Quietly.)* Erasmus—

SOCRATES: *(Hushed tone.)* Shhhh, Augustine, give him time. Each of you took your time. There are many questions that hang like a cloud over us, not just today but always.

HROSTVITHA: True, so true. Socrates, you always have the wisdom we need.

1

AUGUSTINE: Hrostvitha, you always side with him? Why? (*Erasmus groans.*) He was always slow, ever since I noticed him.

AQUINAS: Do you accuse him of being sluggish?

HILLEL: Good words, Aquinas. Let him have peace, as he awakens.

HILDEGARD: "Peace," Hillel. That is the golden word.

HILLEL: Erasmus is turning the final page of his life and opening a new book which is filled with many unknowns. (*Thunder.*)

ERASMUS: (*Stirring, throws off covers, turns to face downstage.*) Voices? Am I hearing voices?

HROSTVITHA: We've been waiting for you.

AUGUSTINE: I've got a bone to pick with Erasmus.

HROSTVITHA: We want to hear from him, first! . . . Don't let your doctrines ruin this moment.

AUGUSTINE: Moment? There are no moments in this room. Just eternity!

HILDEGARD: Peace, I beg you . . . both!

HILLEL: Hildegard, remember this: a single candle can light up a room, but first someone must light the candle.

AUGUSTINE: What does that have to do with him? (*Nods to Erasmus.*)

HILLEL: We all hoped that he could be the light that would solve the riddle between you (*nods to Augustine*) and Aquinas.

AUGUSTINE: Such high hopes only lead to despair.

HILLEL: Even a small step toward illumination will give me hope.

AQUINAS: Augustine, what knocked on your skull today?

AUGUSTINE: This Dutch scholar was one of ours, an Augustinian.

HILLEL: Now he is here with you . . . and us. He will bring new thoughts.

AUGUSTINE: We raised him when he came as an orphan, and his brother. But Erasmus left . . . for money in lecturing.

HILDEGARD: And wounded you? (*Pause.*)

HROSTVITHA: Augustine aims to dispute rather than inquire.

ERASMUS: (*Sitting in the bed.*) Can someone tell me where . . . (*Pause.*)

SOCRATES: You will be with us now, for ages yet to come.

ERASMUS: My old bones . . . (*Moans.*)

AQUINAS: We have been looking forward to meeting you.

HILLEL: Waiting for someone to break the impasse between the two titans of the church.

HROSTVITHA: It's not an impasse for you; you aren't even a member of the church.

HILLEL: Any unsolved riddle creates ripples we all feel, even in our spines.

SOCRATES: Questions, remember we always ask questions. No truths are ever learned from accusations.

AUGUSTINE: Challenges! Truth is gained by making challenges.

AQUINAS: That's why I challenged you, with logic and reason.

ERASMUS: (*Still mystified.*) What has happened? (*Pause.*)

HILLEL: You transitioned.

HILDEGARD: Transformed.

AUGUSTINE: Why did you leave the monastery?

HILDEGARD: This is not the time to bring that up!

ERASMUS: I'm thirsty; I need a good beer. (*All laugh.*)

AQUINAS: No one needs to drink anymore.

HROSTVITHA: When we arrived, Erasmus, we were all thirsty.

SOCRATES: I wasn't.

HROSTVITHA: Consider what you did—

SOCRATES: All I did was take a stand against civil authority because I was committed to the truth and they were not.

AQUINAS: Of course you weren't, Socrates; you had just gulped a goblet of hemlock.

AUGUSTINE: We have crossed over—no more food or drink. Just as the Lord promised. (*Pause.*)

ERASMUS: But no one is singing. I thought there might be singing.

HROSTVITHA: Now and then we do; Hildegard's chants fill this room and explode across the heavens. But not all the time.

ERASMUS: I don't know what's happened. Seems like a splendid dream.

HILLEL: Died, Erasmus, you died.

HILDEGARD: Or it's all a dream. A vision. (*Pause.*)

AQUINAS: Both are like death.

ERASMUS: Death? Humph, that was easy.

AUGUSTINE: When you know there is an eternal reward.

HILLEL: We don't know; we have faith, we believe—

ERASMUS: But earlier . . . I suffered—

HILLEL: Yes, living is hard, death is easy. By the way, I'm Hillel the Elder. (*To Erasmus.*) You've met Socrates and most of our bunch, except maybe Hildegard. You know all of them by their writing, and here they are . . . in this room.

SOCRATES: Enough about belief; we are those who sought the truth—

ERASMUS: (*Surprised.*) The only ones?

AQUINAS: No, no, we are a few from a long list of heavenly ones.

AUGUSTINE: We are among the saints, the near saints, and the not so saintly.

HROSTVITHA: A motley crew that includes weeds along with wheat.

HILLEL: Like a synagogue.

AQUINAS: A university.

HILDEGARD: A kingdom.

SOCRATES: We are the ones who question all things, including what is good, and distinguish it from the non-good.

ERASMUS: Non-good?

HILLEL: I've read your writings; you are one clever soul.

ERASMUS: Thank you, but don't expect cleverness every day. (*Turning toward Socrates.*) And we have all read your works—

SOCRATES: Plato tried to quote me, but the errors he made! I'm still learning, which is why I don't write.

ERASMUS: Saint Socrates, you brought us all closer to the truth.

AUGUSTINE: Saint? A pagan? How did you avoid the eternal fires of Hades?

SOCRATES: I died; I landed in this room. To end my loneliness, I invited each of you to join me.

ERASMUS: (*Looking around, ironically asks.*) Why so few books? (*All laugh.*)

HROSTVITHA: A room without books is like a body without a soul.

ERASMUS: I used to read everything I could. A library is a paradise.

HILLEL: Was. Learn to say "was." A library was—

AUGUSTINE: Who needs a library when you can ask us? (*Pause.*)

SOCRATES: Libraries are full of books we have written.

ERASMUS: But your deeds, Socrates; all of history knows your act of courage.

SOCRATES: What courage?

HILDEGARD: To declare who you are! It can be far from the shores of silence to the waves of speech. The path may be long, and the way is deep. You come to a place where you can no longer walk . . . you must be prepared to leap.

SOCRATES: What is that leap? (*Pause.*) Have any of you—

AUGUSTINE: To abandon the world for the sake of Christ.

ERASMUS: But the irony is your abandonment, as you call it, changed the world.

HROSTVITHA: Your writings, Augustine, your life altered the centuries that followed.

AUGUSTINE: I don't see it . . . what you are telling me—

ERASMUS: No debate. Settled. Except the questions you—

HILDEGARD: (*Intentionally changing the subject.*) Erasmus, you were a terror to the unlawful foolishness of the world.

AQUINAS: I told you that when the time comes, he should join our cluster.

SOCRATES: I'm interested in the question that follows. Do we accept that Augustine shaped the centuries that followed?

ERASMUS: Till Aquinas came along. Then the sparks began to fly.

AUGUSTINE: Does everyone think that?

ERASMUS: Everything I've read speaks of the clashes between you two.

AUGUSTINE: You read the wrong books.

AQUINAS: There aren't any wrong books. Only those we don't approve. Even though they may also contain some truth.

AUGUSTINE: Back to that old argument.

SOCRATES: (*To Erasmus.*) We thought you could resolve the differences between those two (*nods toward Augustine and Aquinas*) once and for all.

ERASMUS: I think I'll let you down. I see the good in everyone, even those I disagree with. So, why resolve differences?

HILDEGARD: And with music, who cares about differences. Music unites us all!

AQUINAS: The Greeks avoid the music of the Romans, and they belittle the music of the Franks, and they all refuse to sing the songs of the Africans.

AUGUSTINE: Another old argument!

HILDEGARD: This could go on for quite some time. Anyone for a cup of tea?

AQUINAS: What is a cup of tea?

HILDEGARD: I don't know. I heard someone say it and it stuck.

ERASMUS: Who has this tea? (*Pause.*) How will we find out what it is?

HILLEL: No one knows. For us it means "quiet time," or "let's change the subject." (*Pause.*)

ERASMUS: I never expected it to be a library.

HROSTVITHA: A library?

ERASMUS: Eternity.

AQUINAS: What a great thought: eternal ideas live in libraries!

HROSTVITHA: It is too cluttered here to be a library!

HILDEGARD: Librarians are far more fastidious than this place—

HROSTVITHA: Organized, you mean organized.

ERASMUS: It feels like home. Books are like family for me.

HROSTVITHA: Of course, like family. They talk but never listen! (*Augustine laughs. Pause.*)

SOCRATES: (*To Hrostvitha.*) And for you, Hrostvitha, what is the meaning of "good"?

HROSTVITHA: First, we need to say where each of us stands. Otherwise, we are setting a trap.

AQUINAS: Are you referring to Teresa?

HROSTVITHA: Teresa of Avila has not hovered near us since you men humiliated her. You (*to Augustine*) set that snare!

AUGUSTINE: Her logic is not logical.

HILLEL: In your eyes—

SOCRATES: If this continues, will she want to come back?

ERASMUS: What do you suggest?

SOCRATES: We return to the unanswered question, "What is good?"

HROSTVITHA: (*To Erasmus.*) We disagree among ourselves, so adding your point of view might add honey to our tea.

HILDEGARD: The essence of wine is in the grape, not in sugar.

AQUINAS: They say the two blend well; the presence of one changes the other.

SOCRATES: What do you have when you blend one good thing with another good thing?

HILDEGARD: Something better.

AUGUSTINE: Logical. Two goods create greater goods. They don't nullify each other. But that will never happen.

HILDEGARD: Obviously, Augustine, the subject is not your cup of tea.

HROSTVITHA: Enough. That's an old retort.

AQUINAS: We have a great question before us, and we always seem to veer away from it. Erasmus, what does it mean to be good?

AUGUSTINE: I thought we agreed not to set a trap for him.

AQUINAS: Ok, I spoke too early.

SOCRATES: Is there ever a time when what is good for the individual is not good for the city?

AUGUSTINE: Do you mean the kingdoms of the world?

AQUINAS: Those that claim to have dominion over our daily living.

SOCRATES: Those are two separate branches on the same tree, but each bears different fruit. Which shall we devour first?

HILLEL: If we are talking about a personal good, I suggest that everyone avoid hating another just because we ourselves don't want to be hated.

AUGUSTINE: That's logical . . . except—

HILLEL: There you go again . . . God's spirit defies logic. Let's pretend that a person down the street hates you. Is it good not to hate him in return?

HILDEGARD: Of course, what good is hate?

HROSTVITHA: If we lived in a world where an eye of hate is traded for an eye, we'd all be blind by now.

HILDEGARD: Many are blind even though their eyes can see.

HROSTVITHA: True, we know them, and some are good, some are lacking goodness.

SOCRATES: So, are they evil . . . if they lack goodness?

HROSTVITHA: Wherever there is an absence of good, evil might fill the vacuum.

ERASMUS: What's a vacuum?

AQUINAS: A lack of air ... discovered after our time.

ERASMUS: Does everyone here know what happened after my time?

AQUINAS: We can see all of it ... if we want to.

AUGUSTINE: But who wants to see it all? The chaos, the suffering, the weeping—

HROSTVITHA: Do you want to see such things now?

ERASMUS: Maybe later. Let me stand here, unchanged, on my ground. (*Others laugh.*) What did I say?

HILDEGARD: We are free of the toil; our being is now in places unknown by those who stand on the ground.

HILLEL: Find a cloud and ride it, we say.

HILDEGARD: Indeed. For as long as you wish.

AQUINAS: Just say, "We stand with eternity."

SOCRATES: That is all interesting, but let's return to the subject. What does "good" mean or what does it mean to "be good"?

HILLEL: Not to be mean is good.

AQUINAS: So, the meaning of "good" is not to be mean? Is that all?

HILLEL: There is more. Immanuel Kant stated—

ERASMUS: Who is Immanuel Kant?

AQUINAS: He came after you.

SOCRATES: Walked in your footsteps.

ERASMUS: I see. Fancy that! I had never heard of him!

HILLEL: Fancy that! You missed a great one, but now you can—

KANT: (*Steps in.*) Did someone call for me?

SOCRATES: Welcome, welcome, Immanuel. Have a seat.

HROSTVITHA: Glad you arrived so quickly.

AQUINAS: Do you know what a cup of tea is?

KANT: Cup of . . . No, I can't say I do.

AQUINAS: We also do not know.

HILLEL: We want to know if you could solve the differences between Augustine and Aquinas. We ask everyone we meet.

KANT: Can't be resolved; forget them and start over!

AUGUSTINE: That is the problem. You threw the two of us into a dustbin.

AQUINAS: Amen to that. But you're a good German; we expect confrontations with you.

KANT: I only did what both of you did earlier: introduce new ways of thinking. New questions.

ERASMUS: That is the essence of learning: new thoughts, new light.

HILLEL: You stated that the absence of good is just that, an absence. Do I understand you correctly? (*Kant nods, approvingly.*)

AUGUSTINE: So, there can't be any bad people. Are there only those who are good and those who are not good? (*Kant nods.*) Then there is no such thing as evil . . . or devils . . . or witches . . . or—

KANT: Evil is the absence of good even if there aren't pitchforks, hot lava, dragons—

AUGUSTINE: Then how do you explain—

SOCRATES: Our friend has made a good point. The absence of good is evil. Anyone want to say more? (*Pause.*) I favor that view.

AUGUSTINE: Of course you would. What do you say, Immanuel? The pagans agree with you?

SOCRATES: The playwrights of my time clearly understood that. Evil deeds by the hero are always upended by the power of goodness, especially when everything looks dire.

AUGUSTINE: There was a time when I also thought so.

AQUINAS: You did!

AUGUSTINE: That evil must run and hide wherever there is good.

HILLEL: The books of Moses stated it correctly. God created all things and declared them to be good. There is no evidence God said, "Some will be good, but others evil."

AUGUSTINE: But there are fallen angels who are the root of all evil.

HILLEL: Figures of speech, symbolic language, full of angels and demons and all sorts of fires and brimstone. But we have other, bigger sharks to fry.

HILDEGARD: Our task is to rescue them from the fall, not to vilify them.

ERASMUS: These are new thoughts . . . Is that what you mean, Immanuel?

KANT: Allow me to state it another way. There is no "bad" art; there only is art which is not good. What some call bad or degenerate art is merely the absence of seeing the goodness that is in it.

HILLEL: That's a new thought; I'll have to jot that down. There are no bad people; only people who are not good.

AUGUSTINE: Where's the logic in that? You deny that the infidel is evil?

KANT: Give me an example.

AUGUSTINE: A man walks down a street and beats another man, a stranger; robs him.

KANT: An evil deed is not the same as an evil being.

AUGUSTINE: Can you not see that an evil deed reveals an evil being?

ERASMUS: You are making a leap in logic. Deeds are actions and temporary; a being has longevity . . . eternal presence—

AQUINAS: A being is rooted in essence; a deed is substance. (*Pause. Thunder.*) And the sum of all thought is in our feelings.

AUGUSTINE: Feelings? Brittle reeds that snap in the wind!

HILDEGARD: Anyone for a cup of tea?

ERASMUS: (*Chuckling.*) What is tea?

AQUINAS: Hate to disappoint you, but that's just a saying we have when someone wants to change the subject. We don't know what tea is.

ERASMUS: So many new things, and Kant brings up new ideas.

KANT: But we are discussing goodness and evil—

AQUINAS: There will be time for that . . . all through eternity.

ERASMUS: So, this is what it's like. No golden avenues, no crosses, and nobody singing choral chants.

AUGUSTINE: The only music worth listening to are the chants of Chrysostom. They can fill a basilica with heavenly goodness.

SOCRATES: You never heard Euripides, did you? All the musicians that followed this Athenian borrowed from him.

AUGUSTINE: How can you believe that?

SOCRATES: You probably never heard him. I did; that is why I believe his music spoke of eternal goodness. (*Pause.*)

HROSTVITHA: Every day brings new surprises. By the way, are you a good actor?

ERASMUS: Me? I probably was . . . before I came here. (*Laughter.*)

AUGUSTINE: So, that's your secret? Acting out your beliefs?

HILDEGARD: You did the same, Augustine, hiding in that cave for how many decades?

AUGUSTINE: I was not hiding. I withdrew from worldliness, and many should consider doing the same as their vocation.

ERASMUS: Tell us more. Why did you view that as the highest form of worship and service?

AUGUSTINE: To live apart and renounce all earthly pleasures.

ERASMUS: My question has two parts. For those who cannot or wish not to hide from earthly delights, are they evil or good?

AUGUSTINE: (*Has been waiting for this moment.*) The world is complicated, and so are the heavens. There is a separation between the kingdom of God and the kingdoms of the world. The first are on the straight and narrow; the second live among the wheat and brambles. They must sort them out, daily.

SOCRATES: Why is that separation necessary?

AUGUSTINE: There is only perfection in the kingdom of God, while the kingdoms of the world are a blend of wheat and weeds, even though few can tell the difference.

KANT: That is an old way of thinking.

AQUINAS: Hush, do you want to have us send you packing?

HILDEGARD: That's what he did to Teresa!

AQUINAS: She gave her life to ecstasy and not to reason.

AUGUSTINE: You are all blinded by the light of passion. (*Thunder.*)

SOCRATES: I'd like to remind all of you: mere mortals do not spring full-blown from the head of Zeus. We are born astride agony and joy. Those are passions!

HILDEGARD: Anyone for a cup of tea?

AUGUSTINE: Not so fast. I am not finished. People in service to the king make compromises and cannot live according to God's perfection. They marry, have children, defend the king's realm with swords and spears. That is God's plan for the world.

ERASMUS: Not all kings deserve to be defended. Even against barbarians.

AUGUSTINE: The barbarians should be put out of their barbaric misery.

ERASMUS: With swords?

AUGUSTINE: Yes, if need be.

ERASMUS: How can there be peace in the world if everyone is dedicated to defending their king against all other kings?

AUGUSTINE: Because that is God's plan for ordering the world. No other way might bring about just results.

AQUINAS: When we speak of justice and just results, we need to remember that the created order has steps one must follow.

ERASMUS: You mean, know the difference between just and unjust wars.

AQUINAS: I have spelled that out in detail, and surely you have read it. (*Pause.*) And agree?

ERASMUS: There is something to be said for things you left out.

AQUINAS: Left out?

ERASMUS: The most chaotic good is always better than any just war!

AUGUSTINE: Every man alive needs to carry a sword in case our enemies march—

ERASMUS: People who are in the world can also refuse to carry the sword.

AUGUSTINE: Cannot be.

ERASMUS: I have met them.

AUGUSTINE: Only heretics refuse the sword.

HROSTVITHA: Let's not be so quick to judge. Say more, Erasmus.

ERASMUS: They refuse to carry the sword and will even die for their belief in God. They trust the Spirit more than they trust iron.

KANT: They often make compromises. What I think is needed for world order is for all the kings to recognize that together they can work toward perpetual peace and avoid continuous warfare.

HILDEGARD: Time for tea, anyone?

ERASMUS: Sounds like a promising idea. (*Pause.*)

KANT: But I had not finished. (*Thunder.*)

ALL except KANT: Time for tea!

SOCRATES: We have to realize that our Immanuel is introducing a new idea that cannot be found among the ancients.

HROSTVITHA: Did you call yourself ancient?

SOCRATES: I'm the oldest person here and have come from the greatest distance.

ERASMUS: Time, from a different time and not distance. Distance is not what it used to be.

AQUINAS: Some say the moon is closer than the sun.

HROSTVITHA: Who would say such a thing?

ERASMUS: An Italian; it's always the Italians!

AUGUSTINE: Since the sun is hotter than the moon—

HROSTVITHA: And brighter.

AUGUSTINE: I believe it is closer. Simple logic.

AQUINAS: But nature is not logical; it does what it wishes!

SOCRATES: Time, space, what difference does it make? The journey was long till I was brought here.

HILDEGARD: You were among the pagans, but your light was brighter than theirs.

AQUINAS: You rose above them.

SOCRATES: That is an odd way to say it. There is no above or below . . . only as we think it to be so.

KANT: Exactly. Such truthful words have never been spoken.

ERASMUS: What makes you so certain?

KANT: There is no religion that cannot be questioned by reason alone. I quote, "Hell is empty, and the devils walk freely on this earth."

HILDEGARD: Who wrote that?

KANT: Someone in England they call the "upstart crow." But his real name was William . . . something.

ERASMUS: When I was in London, they called him Shakeshaft!

KANT: He was a slippery fellow. Yet his poetry is delicate, refined, and among the best.

ERASMUS: You bring innovative ideas. Why have I never heard of you?

KANT: I came to be long after you lived.

ERASMUS: Time. Space! Does anyone understand them?

KANT: Even in this enlightened place we have questions.

AQUINAS: It's simple: one time is all time, one space is all spaces.

ERASMUS: You learned that by watching angels dance on the head of a pin?

AQUINAS: That vision came to me in a dream.

SOCRATES: Again, we are forgetting the topic at hand. What is the nature of good, and how can we know goodness when we see it?

HILLEL: I'll say again, put hate aside and goodness will flow from your hands.

AUGUSTINE: For the monk, it means do unto others as you want them to do toward you.

ERASMUS: Why limit that to monks? Maybe the world needs to do that.

KANT: That's why I wrote, do that which if everyone on earth did it, it would still be called good.

AQUINAS: My dear fellow, that is meaningless because you fail to tell us what "that" is!

KANT: It's indirect, implied, nuanced—

AUGUSTINE: More poetic nonsense. You know we banned such things back when being a believer meant something, but this is . . . (*Pause.*)

KANT: We're waiting.

AUGUSTINE: Monks need certainty; they cannot thrive unless they have discipline.

SOCRATES: We have stumbled onto fruitful ground.

HROSTVITHA: Why do you say monks work and pray each day, and not just pray?

AUGUSTINE: They take strict vows to support their community.

SOCRATES: But do monks keep their vows, always?

AUGUSTINE: Of course, or they leave and renounce their vows.

HILDEGARD: You're forgetting the main thing. Even when the world goes to war, monks do not.

SOCRATES: Is warfare a necessary evil or, as our friend says, "the absence of good"?

AUGUSTINE: Of course it is; that's how heroes are made.

HROSTVITHA: If you live in a monastery and do not go to war yourself, by what authority do you name someone a hero?

AUGUSTINE: Because that is the natural order, a necessity for people who live in the world. There is one God, one Son, one Spirit, one church, and one emperor. We must always remember that and defend those beliefs.

HILDEGARD: And fight?

AUGUSTINE: How would we know the heroes of the age without warriors who win in battle?

HROSTVITHA: Who has made them into heroes? I consider a hero to be one who is compassionate and obedient to God, and that can be accomplished without a sword!

AUGUSTINE: You have conveniently forgotten that God, our God, has established kings, and they prayerfully plan for war and designate who is heroic and who—

ERASMUS: Shall hide in a monastery or far from any city?

AUGUSTINE: What did I hear?

ERASMUS: By making warriors into heroes, you make monks and nuns into cowards.

KANT: I never was a monk.

AQUINAS: Indeed, and you failed to defend just wars!

KANT: A fool's errand, rushing into a just war. When has there ever been a just war?

SOCRATES: My words, nearly. Has there ever been a just war? I'll answer you: the battle at Salamis.

ERASMUS: The Greeks saved their civilization by defeating the Aryans from Persia. Every child knows that.

AQUINAS: That is my first point in just war: it is just to defend your city.

SOCRATES: And your second principle?

AQUINAS: A just war is fought with just means—each side must have equal arms and soldiers.

KANT: That is the problem! Those with greater "means," as you call it, are always the victor.

HILDEGARD: Enough! Hate ignites wars, and apart from Salamis, wars are never just! And even that war is a tale of carnage.

HROSTVITHA: (*Accusatory.*) You men are redefining goodness, and you allow for every smidgen of hate.

SOCRATES: That brings me back to the topic at hand. Must you have goodness to end up with good deeds?

AQUINAS: Yes. In other words, don't destroy your enemy's houses, water, or cattle, which are needed for life and nourishment after the wars.

AUGUSTINE: We believe God ordains kings to declare war, as needed, even if that means total—

KANT: War is not the road to perpetual peace.

AUGUSTINE: Once all the barbarians become Christians, there will be peace.

HROSTVITHA: Till then we should go to war against them?

AUGUSTINE: War is heroic when we take a pagan and battle him to the end.

ERASMUS: But those who commit murder will never have peace.

AQUINAS: We are talking about war, not murder.

ERASMUS: Both are the same, simply different intentions.

AQUINAS: Of course, the intention may be a sin, not the act.

HROSTVITHA: Say that again?

AQUINAS: The pure heart that goes to war is pleasing to God.

KANT: How can you think of such a principle without losing your rational mind? Killing never leads to peace.

HILDEGARD: In the convent we settle differences with prayer, contemplation, and conversation. A violent act never makes for peace. The same is true for times of war.

AUGUSTINE: You are ringing the death knell for the kingdom of God. The kingdom of God exists because the kings of the earthly realm protect it.

AQUINAS: There are many faithful rulers among the earthly realms.

HILDEGARD: How faithful are they if they train their subjects for murder?

AUGUSTINE: My oh my, now I've heard it all. War is not murder; it is the heroic protection of a homeland.

AQUINAS: Obviously, you never read my treatise on just wars.

AUGUSTINE: Or heard of the idea of a holy war?

HILDEGARD: I have read what I've read, heard what I've heard, and know what I know. Men are obsessed with violence; women, with peace.

ERASMUS: (*To Hildegard.*) Hildegard, you are admired for your boldness.

SOCRATES: We have drifted far from understanding goodness. Can we get back to the subject?

KANT: Indeed. Do good intentions justify all deeds, or should the deed be resolved—

(*Pause. Mahatma Gandhi approaches the stage from behind the audience. He walks slowly as those on stage slowly begin to notice. He is casual but focused. Occasionally he stops to greet someone with "prayer" gesture.*)

HILDEGARD: (*As he nears the stage.*) Do you see what I see?

HROSTVITHA: Astonishing. *Mirabilis*! *Mirabilis*. (*Erasmus invites him to sit nearby.*)

AUGUSTINE: How? I mean . . . how? (*Gandhi turns around to gaze on the path he has taken.*)

AQUINAS: *Mirabilis*, indeed!

KANT: That is your argument. Good intentions must be rewarded. (*Gandhi steps onto the stage.*) Welcome, you are welcome.

SOCRATES: Please sit . . . here.

GANDHI: Don't mind if I do. After that long march, I'm—

ALL: Thirsty!

GANDHI: How did you know?

HILDEGARD: We've all said that. (*Pause.*)

GANDHI: What's on the menu?

AQUINAS: Did you ever hear of a cup of tea?

GANDHI: Of course!

AQUINAS: You have!

HILDEGARD: What is it?

GANDHI: The elixir of the gods!

AUGUSTINE: Did I hear . . . gods?

GANDHI: Yes, indeed. Tea, by any other name—

AUGUSTINE: But God is one! One. Three in one!

SOCRATES: For you, of course. Talk about an idea no one understands, three in—

HILDEGARD: (*To Augustine.*) You do not have the answers to all questions. For example, what is tea? (*Augustine shrugs. Pause.*)

GANDHI: It's a health-giving drink made from leaves.

HILDEGARD: Healing?

AQUINAS: Leaves?

GANDHI: Indeed. Leaves from tea trees. Settle the digestion.

KANT: Just leaves and water. (*Gandhi points thumbs up.*) Not a beer? (*Gandhi points thumb down.*)

KANT: Imagine that. Leaves. So, it's a green drink?

GANDHI: No, no—

AQUINAS: Well, I prefer a good Italian wine.

KANT: (*Staring at Gandhi.*) What is your name?

GANDHI: Gandhi. Mahatma Gandhi.

AQUINAS: Mah . . . Mah . . . What did you say?

GANDHI: Mahatma.

AUGUSTINE: How did you find your way here?

GANDHI: I've been walking for a long time. From my Ashram to the sea.

AQUINAS: Why? Why walk so far?

GANDHI: The salt! Boycott salt!

AUGUSTINE: What does that have to do with anything?

GANDHI: Oppose the way the British stole it, forced people into labor, and denied our rights.

HILDEGARD: Welcome, welcome.

GANDHI: Good cheer to each of you!

KANT: A man after my own heart! Walks for justice.

AUGUSTINE: (*Looking at Aquinas.*) How is this possible?

AQUINAS: Maybe while he was studying in London?

GANDHI: Gentlemen and ladies, it is an honor to be in your midst. (*Pause.*)

AUGUSTINE: We need to know, are you . . . within the kingdom? Baptized?

GANDHI: All descriptions depend—

AUGUSTINE: Depend on what?

GANDHI: What you consider to be baptism, because—

AUGUSTINE: It's what God considers, what is written in Scripture!

GANDHI: Yours or mine?

AUGUSTINE: What? What did you say?

GANDHI: We also have scriptures.

AQUINAS: But truth is not spread out evenly among many scriptures; one is superior to the rest. That Scripture happens to be ours.

GANDHI: That may be your belief, but other religions around the world—

AUGUSTINE: We have one sun, one God, and one true religion!

KANT: You are getting too vexed for no reason. Can you shed any light on this, Socrates?

SOCRATES: Zeus in his mercy never—

AUGUSTINE: I think it's time to petition against this. Too many unbaptized assemble here.

KANT: We know you wrote that a Christian's duty is to kill a pagan to get them out of their pagan misery.

SOCRATES: So how did I become so privileged? To be here with you? (*Pause.*) I didn't get baptized; in fact, I don't even remember if I ever took a bath. (*All laugh nervously.*)

AQUINAS and AUGUSTINE: We've asked ourselves that same question.

PART I

KANT: Can't you see? It's obvious.

AQUINAS: No.

HILDEGARD: What does it matter? Goodness is goodness, and Socrates was—

KANT: His death was a sacrifice. An early martyr.

AQUINAS: A martyr for what?

KANT: The truth. For ages you, Socrates, are held up as a model for being a martyr for the truth. I wish our friends understood that.

AUGUSTINE: You make it sound like a journey filled with joy. To die for the truth! As though a pagan would know.

ERASMUS: Augustine, you studied Cicero! Even admired his—

AUGUSTINE: That was different!

AQUINAS: Explain that!

ERASMUS: You honored him as a herald of truth.

AUGUSTINE: It's simple. Cicero was brilliant, and his ideas gave order to my thinking, but I did not accept his religion.

HROSTVITHA: So you can understand that some ancients have much they can teach us.

AUGUSTINE: But I was like a child, and then I gave up childish ways. I then fought for God. I have confessed to it all.

ERASMUS: But you hide behind the walls of an empire and scorn many who give their lives to God.

AUGUSTINE: I do not admire the martyrs, if that is what you mean.

AQUINAS: Only the annoying Anabaptists enjoyed martyrdom.

AUGUSTINE: Well, they were taught a lesson!

ERASMUS: They held tight to what they believed God had called them to do. Even though you and I might consider their actions to be in error, we must admire their devotion.

AUGUSTINE: You are misguided! A heretic is always fully devoted, dedicated to their faulty beliefs.

KANT: It is good to question all things but also realize that there is faith in things unseen.

AUGUSTINE: Spoken like another friend of the Anabaptists!

ERASMUS: I'm curious, are there any here in . . . whatever this is called? Limbo?

AQUINAS: Oh yes, just not in this room.

ERASMUS: Where can I find them?

AQUINAS: They are off to themselves, somewhere else.

ERASMUS: Typical.

AQUINAS: Why do you ask?

ERASMUS: Just wondered if they also found heavenly bliss.

AUGUSTINE: Don't call this heaven!

ERASMUS: Why not?

AUGUSTINE: There are baptized and unbaptized up here, so it can't be heaven.

AQUINAS: You will never change, will you!

AUGUSTINE: What does that mean?

ERASMUS: Let me put it this way: you go to confession, don't you?

AUGUSTINE: Of course.

ERASMUS: Have you ever confessed to your, umm, ahh . . .

KANT: "Disgust" is the word you need.

ERASMUS: Disgust toward those who hold other beliefs? (*Pause.*)

HROSTVITHA: If your religion does not lead you to compassion toward others, especially the downtrodden ones, what's the purpose for religion?

AUGUSTINE: Heaven! It's all about heaven!

AQUINAS: It's about earth! Life on earth! Then wait for heaven.

KANT: It's now or never; no need to wait!

HILDEGARD: Time for tea, anyone! (*All laugh.*)

HROSTVITHA: Look around you. Who's still waiting for heaven?

KANT: And it's rather pleasant, most of the time.

AQUINAS: At least the insurrectionist Martin Luther isn't here.

AUGUSTINE: He defied the pope.

AQUINAS: Then he ignited wars against our church.

ERASMUS: Maybe we can all agree on that, except our friend Immanuel.

ALL except KANT: Agreed!

KANT: May I say why I withheld—

AQUINAS: Because Luther speaks for you.

KANT: I speak for myself. He spoke for himself.

AUGUSTINE: Why mention that rebel?

KANT: It was not Luther but Rome that lit the flame that led to his awakening.

AQUINAS: Why isn't he here? He should be here to speak for himself.

KANT: His light was bright, hot, when the rest of the world faded.

AUGUSTINE: I'd like to put him back into a monastery.

HILDEGARD: Because of you, he's stayed away.

KANT: Luther had good intentions. He employed reason as his defense.

AUGUSTINE: I always thought you betrayed the truth; now I know why.

AQUINAS: But do you see any good in Luther's rebellious ideas?

KANT: What is rebellion to some is reformation to others. There is value in his insights.

ERASMUS: I, too, don't hold Luther in high esteem; in fact, I have been harsh with him. But many consider him worthy—

AUGUSTINE: He is an insurrectionist cur and completely unworthy—

AQUINAS: He disgraced his station in life.

KANT: He established one truth beyond all else. That the church can survive theological divisions and even be renewed.

AUGUSTINE: Such words have never been spoken before, here, in my presence.

KANT: They have now. For this new way of looking at truth, we must thank Erasmus. He posed and answered so many probing questions, he is a Christian Socrates.

AUGUSTINE: Too many questions. Also misguided more than once. Once you spoke in favor of the demands drafted by that firebrand from the Teutonic tribes.

AQUINAS: It began with that. First, Sebastian's moaning over peasant suffering, then the twelve petitions, and then a clarion call for revolution. It's always the same: first the call for peace, then a march for justice, and finally the call to arm the peasants. That is how it happened.

ERASMUS: It is one thing to champion the poor; it is altogether another to give them arms to revolt.

AQUINAS: You mean boiling oil tossed by catapults?

KANT: Muskets! Pitchforks! They were crushed in a fortnight.

ERASMUS: I didn't join the rebellion, although they had some valid points.

AQUINAS: And they are not vile to you?

ERASMUS: The nobles have squeezed the poor off their land, their livelihood. They had nothing to eat. Their earnings are not enough to pay rent. They are treated like slaves but given the innocuous title "serfs." Slaves who refused to fight, died; slaves who fought for their masters, died. No one can say that was good.

AQUINAS: But the Scripture says, "Slaves obey—"

AUGUSTINE: God ordained the earthly kingdoms, and what the kings do has God's blessing. Think about that. All of you think about that. Slaves, obey your masters.

KANT: That was true in my day. Especially in America.

GANDHI: You know about America?

KANT: I know about the revolution.

GANDHI: Too many died . . . just to free half the people.

AQUINAS: Oh really? I haven't paid attention.

GANDHI: No one usually does.

KANT: Does what?

GANDHI: Pay attention to that half of the world which isn't free.

AQUINAS: Are you accusing men? A priest? For not paying attention?

GANDHI: We are all in good company. Half the world is awake; the other half slumbers.

AQUINAS: And the Americans have slumbered?

KANT: No, they wrote such noble ideals. All people are created with rights, equality, and liberty—

GANDHI: They are an odd bunch.

KANT: Who?

GANDHI: The Americans.

KANT: Are you saying they are not living up to their own principles?

GANDHI: Who knows how they do it—White, Black, and nameless others.

HROSTVITHA: What is that supposed to mean?

GANDHI: You just wait until you meet one. Your eyes will pop out. Mine did.

(*Quick blackout.*)

Intermission

(*Hildegard von Bingen music during intermission.*)

Part II

(Lights slowly rise to reveal all on stage but in different areas than at the end of part I.)

AQUINAS: What were we talking about?

KANT: Before that storm interrupted us?

AQUINAS: Yes.

ERASMUS: I never expected there might be storms here.

GANDHI: Did an American stop by while it was dark?

KANT: I didn't see anyone. Why?

GANDHI: Just asking.

AQUINAS: You suspicious soul; you think an American did that?

KANT: Stop the lights in the universe?

GANDHI: No, no. No country is that powerful.

AUGUSTINE: But you think they might, someday?

GANDHI: Who can know the place, the day, the hour? *(Pause.)*

HROSTVITHA: Before the unexplained disorder, we were discussing the Scripture.

AQUINAS: Oh yes, the Scripture says, "Slaves, obey your—"

AUGUSTINE: I know that one. God ordained the earthly kingdoms, and what the kings do has God's blessing. Think about that. All of you think about that. Slaves, obey your masters.

31

ERASMUS: Some may have been corrupted by that doctrine, believing the crown makes all things right.

AQUINAS: But if they are fed, clothed, and housed within the land, how can we, the penniless ordained, come to their aid?

AUGUSTINE: You raise questions that are outside the realm of the church. We work on spiritual matters.

ERASMUS: The well-being of all, including women, is a spiritual matter.

HILDEGARD: Our new friend is full of wisdom.

KANT: Erasmus, the Christian Socrates! And here they are, together.

HROSTVITHA: That is good.

AUGUSTINE: Everyone talks about what is good. But we never discuss what is evil . . . those things we need to avoid. If you seek the kingdom of God, you will never face the demons of the world.

KANT: I have seen Asian ceramics and know that great art is being created around the world, and therefore many good people exist wherever they live. But then, maybe the Germans are the best . . . in God's eyes.

AUGUSTINE: Impossible. A bunch of ruffians marching across the earth are pleasing to God?

HILLEL: Be careful, Immanuel, he can't take a joke!

KANT: I have studied Japanese vases, and they tell a different story. Being good is the foundation for good living and for good art. All religions teach good living. The artist is telling us that.

HROSTVITHA: In my convent the sisters copied books and decorated the margins. They were beautiful. Each and every one left me with a sense of awe. What have these women wrought? The Divine was present in each meticulous word they wrote.

KANT: Beauty is universal. It is a gift given to each person to see in their own way.

HROSTVITHA: That is a valid point. The Roman slave Terence from Africa did just that. His plays are the best, and he never knew Christ.

ERASMUS: Goodness, goodness resides in all of us, and it's how we put it to work that matters.

HILLEL: That is a worthy thought. I might write a new scroll on that.

ERASMUS: The bishop of Rome has widened his shoulders to recognize the Augustinians, Dominicans, Benedictines, Franciscans, and who knows how many others there might be, so why can't they open their arms to embrace the new voices who seek a higher level of—

KANT: And vows to an order do not become paths to grace. Martin Luther stood on that and did not change.

AUGUSTINE: Heretics! Heretics! All of you! I don't see how you even entered this room! Out! Out! (*Pause. All ignore him.*)

HROSTVITHA: (*After everyone's nervous pause.*) What does our friend from India say?

KANT: You've been so quiet. (*Pause.*)

GANDHI: I read the Sermon on the Mount many times. I was touched by the kindness of Jesus. The whole sermon is about establishing peace in the world. I still believe that a follower of God who lives according to the Sermon on the Mount is in the hands of the eternal one.

ERASMUS: Here we have a Jew and a Hindu among Christians from different orders, and we can converse with each other, peacefully.

HILDEGARD: Peacefully?

AQUINAS: Might be true here, but too idealistic for the masses.

AUGUSTINE: Agreed. Plant those ideas in the minds of the public, chaos will erupt. It would be the end of civilization as we know it.

SOCRATES: According to your Christ, surely everyone can have peaceful disagreements on this. That's how I lived. It's why I invited you here.

AQUINAS: You invited us? Why?

SOCRATES: Because this is the room where it happens.

HROSTVITHA: Where did you find that phrase?

SOCRATES: Heard it somewhere, maybe from a guy from Macedonia.

HROSTVITHA: But why us . . . (*counting*) nine . . . and two empty chairs?

SOCRATES: Here we discover new truths from new ones to arrive. I heard something today: nonviolence can be the best strategy for opposing injustice. That is like music to my ears. (*Drumroll.*)

KANT: He is on the right road toward perpetual peace.

AUGUSTINE: I know why.

HROSTVITHA: Why?

AUGUSTINE: You are both pagans.

KANT: And who gives anyone the authority to judge the difference? Not any of us here, not any of us.

ERASMUS: Isn't it time we ask someone how they have lived and not what they believed? (*Long pause.*)

HROSTVITHA: Did I hear a pin drop?

HILDEGARD: I did.

AQUINAS: Erasmus, you sound like an anarchist . . . Remember what the Romans did to Jerusalem?

KANT: And the bishops to Münster!

AUGUSTINE: There is only one God and one king. The bishop of Rome and the king of the empire are God's voices on earth. That is written into the very nature of the universe. Otherwise, the way our friend from India speaks, there will be anarchy and bloodshed.

GANDHI: It was not like that at all. The invaders were on our roads, in our gardens, our fields, and we were taking them back from them. The people marched and threw off the English empire.

SOCRATES: (*Laughing.*) I had students who thought they could destroy an empire!

KANT: We have all seen them in one class or another. (*Pause.*)

HILDEGARD: That helped to pass the time. Thanks, Mr. Gandhi.

ALL: Yes, yes, thank you. (*Pause.*)

SOCRATES: We need to explore further the essence of goodness. Our new friend from India has given us a political lesson. But there are other ways to look at goodness. I think of the arts and how we decide what is good. But who can decide whether a painting or music happens to be good or fail to be good?

AUGUSTINE: We know that when music is good it doesn't have words and avoids discord.

SOCRATES: Why no words?

AUGUSTINE: Unless they are directly from the Scriptures. All the rest is polluted by the mind from which it springs.

SOCRATES: Then you condemn the operas of my day, *Oedipus, Antigone, Agamemnon,* as useless bits of pleasure?

AUGUSTINE: They are a testament to human chaos and failure. Music needs to be soothing, sublime. Who wants to be Oedipus? Agamemnon?

HROSTVITHA: You didn't mention *Antigone.*

AUGUSTINE: For a particularly good reason: I cannot make up my mind about that one.

SOCRATES: She obeyed God rather than the king.

AQUINAS: Makes her an early Anabaptist without the baptism. Misguided heretics. She disobeyed the king, and the king is God's ordained in the world for the purpose of establishing order among people.

KANT: That is wishful thinking. We are not following the challenge Socrates gave us. What is art, and who can decide its value?

AUGUSTINE: I said my piece.

HILDEGARD: All art is divine, and no one can judge. We have a variety of tastes.

KANT: What are those tastes? Is your taste better than mine? Who can tell?

HROSTVITHA: In my estimation Terence of Rome is the best playwright.

HILLEL: Maybe not. There is nothing like the books of Moses to see the drama of the human saga.

HROSTVITHA: They are great narratives, but who can perform them? As written.

AQUINAS: Our friend Hillel always surprises us with something new.

HROSTVITHA: Terence penned excellent characters, ideas that will challenge any philosopher. He gave us moral lessons and flawless plots. He is the best playwright of all time.

SOCRATES: Better than Euripides? He was the greatest of all time.

HROSTVITHA: We didn't know about him or the other ancients, except for that scoundrel Seneca and the mindless bits by Plautus.

SOCRATES: The Greeks? Tragedies, comedies, the theater in Athens? The best in the world. You never heard about them?

HROSTVITHA: Maybe some have, but they were unknown in my day.

SOCRATES: Do you mean forgotten?

AUGUSTINE: Oh yes, we killed those hedonistic festivals. The church and theater are at each other's throats. One lives; the other dies.

AQUINAS: At each other's throats? Too harsh. In my day, the church again produced plays, in cathedrals. What can you add, Hrostvitha?

HROSTVITHA: I've been laughing inside! I wrote plays! The convent staged them again and again. Many were copied and sold.

ERASMUS: Your plays are excellent for teaching morality. The faithful always benefit from your wisdom.

AUGUSTINE: The kingdoms of the world are not worthy of our attention, and we should not imitate what they do, even their gaudy entertainments. Ban them. Ban them all. That's why I withdrew and formed a true community behind walls that shut out all that noise. Today, the family of God is broken.

KANT: There is no need to shed a tear; criticism leads to greater faithfulness.

ERASMUS: My thoughts exactly! Have you read my books?

KANT: Everyone reads them. Classics for all time.

AUGUSTINE: Our skeptic has become a classic.

GANDHI: I, a Hindu, also read Erasmus. Brilliant questions for any religious soul.

HROSTVITHA: Seems like all the great ones came after my time.

ERASMUS: Not at all. The advantage we had is that you lit the torch that led us forward.

KANT: Yet, all that publishing has not stopped wars, pestilence, hunger—

HILDEGARD: Publish or not, where there is no vision, the people perish.

AQUINAS: Very few in my circle of Dominicans are concerned about war or pestilence.

ERASMUS: Another reason to read the Anabaptists.

GANDHI: Do they follow the Sermon on the Mount?

ERASMUS: More than most others.

GANDHI: That is food for thought. (*Pause.*) Here we are . . . with Erasmus.

KANT: Indeed.

GANDHI: A light to all nations.

KANT: He stood alone much of the time. But he did not hide.

HILDEGARD: Erasmus walked the music of the spheres.

SOCRATES: He understood the nature of the good. The arts instill good behavior because they have the power to touch the soul. Yet everyone's obsession is with war, destruction. Why are we humans like that?

KANT: Think of it this way: there is a connection between the fine arts and goodness. We need more of one, less of the other.

HROSTVITHA: Yes, we learn goodness from our teachings and with tradition. Otherwise, there would be chaos everywhere.

AUGUSTINE: Barbaric anarchy because they rebel against the truth.

HILLEL: Have you learned nothing since you arrived here?

AUGUSTINE: The highest good is found in the sacraments, and they are redemptive for all souls. Without baptism, the Eucharist, the Mass, and the bishop of Rome, we would all descend into hell itself.

ERASMUS: Every barbarian, as you call them, deserves our love, not our anger.

HILDEGARD: And you, Immanuel, you know this subject. Tell us.

KANT: Indeed, and my ideas are more nuanced than what we have heard so far. I don't say they are in error, but I have developed a more complex system.

GANDHI: You'll have to explain it to us. Many, myself included, have read your books, but few understand them.

KANT: No individual can see a play and judge whether is it good or not. They may really like it and declare it to be good, but that doesn't make it so. Goodness is a quality that cannot be determined by one person, one community, one country alone since subjective judgments are seldom universal calculations. That is this philosopher's view.

AUGUSTINE: But your philosophy cannot save us—

HILDEGARD: Music can. Music can send the soul to great heights, and it transforms life itself. Everything we know . . . Even Augustine and Aquinas yield to the rhythms of the heart. The heart is like a lute: when plucked, it rises to the heavens.

AUGUSTINE: Only music of the church can do that. The wandering minstrels with their ditties are corrupting the youth.

KANT: I enjoy a rousing beer hall melody, and so did Martin Luther.

AUGUSTINE: Not that villain again!

HILDEGARD: Every song nurtures a feeling that is divine. When Susanne Langer plays piano, you know it is her soul speaking to you.

AUGUSTINE: The faithful cannot, should not, yield to their feelings. Because in Adam's fall we stumbled also.

HILDEGARD: Music redeems our souls by stirring our feelings.

AUGUSTINE: Only the music of the church and its great teachings will do that.

KANT: But you, my friend, inspired these questions with your long book *The City of God*. You created a perfect contrast between the Divine and the human. A dualism.

AQUINAS: Dualism?

KANT: Finding the truth by setting up opposites. The Greek poets did it best: the kings of this world in a struggle with the powers of the gods. That is at the root of all their tragedies.

HROSTVITHA: That is in your book?

KANT: That is what I tried to say.

HILDEGARD: But how do you teach goodness so that all, and not just the powerful, will enjoy its harvests?

KANT: If you understand a good work of art, you will understand good in human behavior. Observing someone do a good deed touches the soul as much as a complex composition by Mozart.

SOCRATES: Or Euripides!

HROSTVITHA: And you believe that?

KANT: Indeed.

HROSTVITHA: I do too. Maybe I have found my soul's companion.

AUGUSTINE: My oh my.

KANT: Goodness in the arts helps us understand other categories of goodness in human feeling. Good feelings drive our lives towards good—

LANGER: (*Entering.*) Did someone say "feelings"? (*They all point to Kant.*) It woke me from my slumber.

HILDEGARD: Welcome, Susanne, you are welcome.

HROSTVITHA: Langer. Susanne Langer. I've been waiting to meet you. I'm Hrostvitha and this is Hildegard.

HILDEGARD: Welcome Susanne, welcome to the luminaries.

LANGER: It's my honor to meet you! Your music lifts every soul. Hrostvitha, you are new to me.

HROSTVITHA: The same is true for everyone. My work is not remembered.

AQUINAS: Plays, our Hrostvitha wrote plays, and I also welcome you, Susanne.

ERASMUS: Susanne, have you ever heard of a "cup of tea"?

LANGER: Of course, Earl Grey is the best.

AQUINAS: Gray? Hot water becomes gray?

LANGER: Oh no, it's brown.

KANT: Let me understand this. A cup of tea is a drink that is brown but it is called gray?

LANGER: It's not named gray. It's label is Black Pekoe.

AQUINAS: What? Black?

LANGER: (*Laughs.*) Of course.

AUGUSTINE: That is not logical!

AQUINAS: If I understand you, tea is brown but is called black or gray and is made from green leaves?

AUGUSTINE: That's like calling a rock a fish! (*All laugh.*)

KANT: When language no longer means what it says, then—

AUGUSTINE: How could anyone ever tell the difference between a black book and a brown book!

HROSTVITHA: Anyone for a cup of tea!

GANDHI: (*To Kant.*) I hear there's more beer in Germany than all the tea in China.

KANT: I'll drink to that!

HILLEL: That line is not worth the parchment it's scribbled on.

LANGER: It's the brand for Grey's tea, and everyone knows it.

KANT: Brand?

LANGER: All of you are known by your brand. Yours, Immanuel, might be "reason" because everyone associates that with you. And you, Augustine, a Platonist from your *City of God*; Aquinas, the empiricist; Erasmus, the inquirer; Hrostvitha the moralist; Hildegard the visionary; and—

AUGUSTINE: What? Are we reduced to one-word labels?

ERASMUS: No, no, I reject all labels, all attempts to identify me with a phrase.

KANT: We are human beings, not brands!

HILDEGARD: Now are we ready for a cup of tea? (*Laughter.*)

AQUINAS: But words cannot say anything except what they mean until we suddenly learn that black is brown and also gray.

SOCRATES: And you, Susanne, what brings you into this room?

LANGER: I am Susanne Langer. What brought me into this room? I don't really know, but I heard the word "feelings" in a dream, and it woke me up.

AQUINAS: A dream? (*Langer nods.*) Not very rational . . . to follow a dream.

LANGER: Oh, don't worry. Our minds respond to certain words, and they trigger deep feelings, and deep feelings are at the root of our logical thinking. Long before we have words for an idea, we have feelings.

HILDEGARD: Truer words were never spoken. We can now explain what I have known but could not say with words, only with my music.

AQUINAS: You sang what your heart already knew? I also know that. When I look up at a stained glass window, I'm filled with awe. The words come later.

KANT: First, the essence of feeling, which is followed by the substance we know as knowledge. That is the moment we learn goodness in art and goodness in humanity.

AQUINAS: I'm trying to jot down these new thoughts. Go on with—

KANT: There are three kinds of art. Mechanical arts that give us buildings and carriages. Decorative arts that add color and shape to things we make. And then, then, there is that genius who does fine art by adding feelings to a work of art.

SOCRATES: But does it shed light on goodness?

KANT: Good art enlightens our understanding of human goodness.

AQUINAS: Did you hear that, Augustine? The division between us is erased with one brief axiom.

AUGUSTINE: Hardly anyone has said any kind words to me. I think I'll go back to my cave.

LANGER: We no longer see great divisions between sacred and secular because we are more alike than unalike.

KANT: Knowledge by revelation or experience are both paths to truth.

AUGUSTINE: That is too complicated. There is religious art on one side and secular art on the other, with nothing in between.

ERASMUS: I tend to think otherwise. Ever listen to a folk singer? Their so-called secular art inspires awe in many.

KANT: Art needs to elicit feelings and not just look good. To elicit feelings with paint and a brush is the work of a genius.

AQUINAS: Genius? Hmmm. A new word.

ERASMUS: But what does it mean?

KANT: The artist who evokes feelings in a way no other artist has done before. That takes a genius.

ERASMUS: But can all such feelings be called "good"?

LANGER: The arts, especially music, shape our feelings, and our feelings provide order for our lives.

AUGUSTINE: The greatest art relies on the word of God as revealed in Scripture. We are grateful for the Emperor Constantine who made the empire safe for the church to flourish.

KANT: Did you say Constantine? Grateful?

HILDEGARD: Of course. Without him my sisters in the convent would not be there.

HROSTVITHA: Mine too! Otherwise, they would be shackled to men.

AQUINAS: But you aided them but did not take vows—

HROSTVITHA: The gifts to my sisters spoke for my heart more than any vows ever could.

KANT: Even in a convent there are levels of commitment. That was the genius of Luther.

AUGUSTINE: The followers of Luther ruin every good thought, corrupt every good deed. Sacred gifts have made the church thrive. As soon as the coin in the coffer rings, the soul—

KANT: Stop it. Do you want the *Ninety-Five Theses* of Luther thrown at you? Again?

HILLEL: That was harsh. I thought you were a reasonable man.

HILDEGARD: A piercing mind can throw sharp quills. (*Pause.*)

KANT: All the Reformers used a lot of ink.

AQUINAS: Name Luther if you wish, just don't have us hear about the Anabaptists and their—

ERASMUS: They are faithful even unto martyrdom.

AUGUSTINE: Time and again you put your finger in the dike to protect them.

AQUINAS: More than a finger, this time, his whole arm.

HILLEL: What does our new friend say to that?

ERASMUS: I was never rebaptized because once is enough . . . for those who believe it is a sacrament. Twice does not add a jot or tittle to one's salvation.

AQUINAS: Well said.

HILLEL: Why do you all insist upon baptism?

AQUINAS: For the salvation of your soul.

AUGUSTINE: To gain eternal life.

ERASMUS: There is more to the ritual than that.

KANT: I want to hear that again.

ERASMUS: It's a ritual that sums up your commitment to the congregation of the faithful.

GANDHI: That poses a great question. No one . . . or no one from around the world can be considered faithful unless they are baptized?

ERASMUS: Do you dispute that?

GANDHI: Not really. In India we all are supposed to dip in the Ganges, at least once. My parents made sure I was dunked, completely.

AQUINAS: (*To Augustine, who remains silent.*) I'd like to hear your argument against that.

SOCRATES: How can we say that one dip in the river here is baptism and another is not?

AQUINAS: Because it must be administered by a priest.

GANDHI: A Hindu priest dunked me!

HILLEL: Was your Jesus baptized by a priest?

AUGUSTINE: That was different.

GANDHI: You admit there are differences, but the Ganges is invalid? (*Pause.*)

LANGER: If dipping in a river symbolizes belonging to a tradition, then the Ganges is good enough for me.

AQUINAS: (*Vexed.*) But that is not the same thing! (*Pause.*)

HILDEGARD: Anyone for Earl Grey tea called black but is brown? (*All laugh.*)

ERASMUS: Surely you have heard that a rose by any other name is still a rose.

GANDHI: And can smell so sweet.

HILLEL: (*Writing.*) That is one of the best lines I've ever heard. How can anyone ever improve on that?

AUGUSTINE: None of you have mentioned that knowledge comes not from experience but by revelation. All divine truths known on earth have been revealed to us.

AQUINAS: Did you ever consider the great cathedrals and their tinted windows? When you experience how invisible light becomes visible with color, it is a divine moment. An experience like no other.

LANGER: That is the long debate, isn't it fellows? You will never bridge that chasm without considering another dimension. A revelation is a fantasy unless it is grounded in feeling, and experience without new insights, thoughts, is mere indulgence. It is the depth of feeling that guides both experience and revelation into enlightenment. (*Pause.*)

ERASMUS: Langer, those are bold words.

SOCRATES: And worthy of discussion.

ERASMUS: Are you saying that revelation and experience is useless unless they are guided by feelings?

LANGER: All thoughts, all insights, arise because feelings give them shape.

AQUINAS: Even our knowledge of God?

LANGER: That is far afield from my consideration.

KANT: I've thought about it. Mulled over it for years. Our knowledge of God may come by revelation. But even then, it only becomes meaningful after it is experienced. And experience can be a sense of awe or something mundane.

AQUINAS: That is the problem, isn't it? Much of life is mundane.

GANDHI: The problem is this . . . none of you ever got married. That's the end of mundane.

LANGER: I did. I knew where to look because otherwise, you end up with another hound dog.

AQUINAS: What?

LANGER: Sorry, just a saying.

AUGUSTINE: I'm listening and what I'm hearing is disturbing. The only source for knowledge is revelation, and all of you make it sound as though it also comes by way of human experience.

HILLEL: The law and the prophets mean nothing unless they are lived, alive in us.

AUGUSTINE: Of course you would say that!

GANDHI: The world did not see what England did, until we showed them how their boots were on our necks.

HROSTVITHA: Writing a play about suffering is one thing; to experience it in performance is a new path to the truth.

LANGER: When we feel pain, we learn quickly.

KANT: (*To Langer.*) Are you saying that experience of a play is the foundation for knowing the truth? All the rest is a dream. Am I saying that correctly?

LANGER: So far, so good. All knowledge begins as feeling.

AUGUSTINE: All of you . . . why are you in this room? Because I did expect more respect from each of you. But now this! Feelings! Makes my arse sore! (*Chuckling from group.*)

AQUINAS: If it makes you sore, maybe it's time to stop riding the same camel. (*Laughter.*)

AUGUSTINE: Leave! I ask you to leave. (*Pause.*) Now! Heretics, all! (*No one leaves.*) Here I am with a skeptic, professor of theology, a Hindu, a Jew, and a Lutheran scoundrel—

LANGER: Two scoundrels.

AUGUSTINE: Two Lutherans! Who thought this might work?

KANT: Your dream of a unified church with one bishop ruling all is an impossible dream. It lacks reason.

AUGUSTINE: But I can lament, can't I? (*Pause. Hildegard comforts him.*)

GANDHI: The world is a large place and the heavens even greater. I'll find another abode for my eternal journey. (*Along with Hillel, begins toward the exit.*)

HILDEGARD: Please don't leave. Stay. Maybe cooler heads will soon prevail.

AUGUSTINE: Nice words, but all of you are on a twisting path to Hades.

KANT: Now that is almost laughable.

AUGUSTINE: Why?

KANT: Because we are all searching for the truth until your dualism—

SOCRATES: Hush, everyone. Who knew that discussions on art could be so contentious.

AUGUSTINE: That's because all these guests have sold their soul to that Aristotle and his empiricism and have abandoned Plato, the one true thinker.

SOCRATES: Snap judgements such as that need to be challenged.

KANT: We are not criticizing Plato, but neither are we repeating Aristotle. We are ploughing new ground. With his careful reasoning, Erasmus led us down that road.

HILLEL: The same was said of Jesus, but it didn't take long for his followers to settle into the old ways of doing things. An eye for an eye, a sword for a sword.

SOCRATES: Not war again. Please, let's settle this. What does art have to do with feeling, and what do feelings have to do with human action?

HILDEGARD: I know I only do what feels right, and afterwards I contemplate on my actions.

AQUINAS: That is true for everyone. Even my friend standing next to me.

AUGUSTINE: I will speak for myself, thank you. I, too, lived as a hedonist in my youth but gave up those ways when God revealed himself to me. Then I followed the path toward holiness.

ERASMUS: And that path led to your monastic life where you then condemned your earlier dissipation—

AUGUSTINE: I did give up—

ERASMUS: Do you want to divide the world between the fallen who cannot achieve purity and separate them from the holy ones? (*Pause.*) Why divide the world between the righteous and the unrighteous? Today we see things through darkened windows, but someday we will—

AUGUSTINE: The ideals in the Sermon on the Mount can be lived by those set apart from worldly powers. The rest exist amid the wheat and thorns. They follow two masters.

GANDHI: (*Making amends.*) That is noble and honorable. I was also a fish floundering on the beach until the idea came to me, maybe a revelation, that the Satyagraha, our scripture, is the path to truth.

HILLEL: The ancients are worth reading even though they lived ages ago. The truth transcends time.

HROSTVITHA: That was my experience too. I lived a life of wealth, privilege, and luxury until one day I saw how I was wasting my time. So, I joined a convent and managed it well.

KANT: All of you talk about goodness and link it with religion. Maybe goodness can be learned even by those who have no religion.

AQUINAS: Impossible.

AUGUSTINE: Agreed! Impossible. Without the one true God, we are lost.

HILLEL: Glad you included me in that circle.

AUGUSTINE: What? What did I say?

HILLEL: I also would be lost without God. (*Augustine shakes his head, puzzled. Sound of soft rain.*)

HILDEGARD: But God is everywhere, even where I fear to go.

ELVIS: (*The American. Slowly ambles downstage from the chairs and tables. After a slow stroll and gazing in all directions.*) This jailhouse rocks!

AUGUSTINE: (*Snapping.*) This is not a jailhouse!

ELVIS: Well, don't be cruel.

AQUINAS: Who invited him?

ELVIS: Sooner or later, you'll see, I'm just a big hunk 'o love.

HROSTVITHA: (*Also suspicious.*) Not so fast. Were you ever baptized?

ELVIS: Oh yeah, down by the river.

KANT: Seriously, why did you come here?

ELVIS: I felt the early morning rain, and—

AUGUSTINE: (*Still hostile.*) But who let you in . . . here, with us?

ELVIS: Don't get all shook up over me. Sooner or later, you'll love me tender.

HROSTVITHA: But why? Us? Why come here?

ELVIS: It's now or never; no one can wait!

Augustine: (*Groans.*) I've heard that already!

ELVIS: I look at all of you, especially this guy (*gestures toward Gandhi*), and I can't help falling in love.

KANT: (*In challenge.*) What does a person like you know of love? (*Pause.*)

ELVIS: (*Looks at audience.*) The early morning rain stopped; it is time for me step farther along where I'll understand why. (*In silence he crosses the stage. Looks at Langer, holds out his hand to her, she turns away.*) I feel my temperature rising . . . You are always on my mind! (*Holds out his hand again. Slowly exits. Rain slowly fades.*)

KANT: How many of those are we going to see?

HROSTVITHA: Where did he come from?

GANDHI: Now you've met one. A typical one.

HILDEGARD: An American?

GANDHI: Bingo!

AQUINAS: (*Confused.*) Bingo?

GANDHI: Just a saying. Learned it from an American.

LANGER: (*Laughing.*) You don't need to know. It's complicated.

HROSTVITHA: Must be a lot of odd ducks there.

GANDHI: Many showed up along the Ganges.

HROSTVITHA: Dressed like that?

GANDHI: No, no, I meant Americans. (*Hildegard laughs.*)

HILDEGARD: He thought this was a jailhouse.

ALL: That's right.

HILDEGARD: He knows nothing, nothing at all about being confined.

AUGUSTINE: Or about the loving hand of God.

AQUINAS: Augustine, that doesn't sound like you.

AUGUSTINE: Yes, it does, I have felt it guide me.

HILDEGARD: Where have you been hiding this?

LANGER: (*Far stage right. Begins laughing quietly.*)

ERASMUS: (*At stage left.*) Do I hear laughter . . . coming from—

HILDEGARD: (*Near Erasmus.*) I hear it too.

KANT: Laughter? I don't think I did. I was too disturbed by this fellow.

ERASMUS: Langer, what has happened?

HROSTVITHA: Tell us why laughter.

LANGER: (*Laughter subsides.*) I met him. Once.

KANT: That clown?

LANGER: Yes, that clown!

HILDEGARD: How?

LANGER: He came to the university. To perform. He was walking down a corridor. Lost. I gave him directions to the washroom. It was urgent. (*They all begin to laugh. Even Kant.*)

KANT: So, he recognized you? Remembered you?

LANGER: I don't know.

HILDEGARD: He wanted to greet you.

LANGER: He was like a bridge over troubled waters then and still is so.

KANT: Just remember: where love is, there is God also.

AUGUSTINE: Where did you find that?

KANT: Just a saying.

GANDHI: A Russian, a Russian wrote that.

AQUINAS: Not possible. Not in that unlettered country.

GANDHI: In honor of the Anabaptists.

AQUINAS: Not them again!

ERASMUS: They seem to be swarming everywhere, even in Russia.

HILDEGARD: Whoever spreads God's love should go anywhere they please. Even to Russia.

KANT: Does anyone actually know what is going on in Russia? (*Silence. Pause.*) That answers that.

SOCRATES: Back to our clown. Langer, he will find you again. He held out his hand once, twice; he'll hold it out again.

LANGER: I know, I know. That's why laughter rose from deep within. I know he'll return.

AQUINAS: Is this what your books are about?

ERASMUS: (*To Langer.*) Feelings? Laughter. We all certainly felt something . . . even without his hand reaching out.

LANGER: He has that effect on people. Some start screaming the minute they see him. I don't understand it.

KANT: I don't, that's certain.

ERASMUS: Many admired him?

LANGER: The masses, the hoards, flocked to him. He had this magic touch.

SOCRATES: His hand, he reached out—

ERASMUS: I thought death would end all that.

HILDEGARD: For some, maybe.

SOCRATES: But each in our own unique way when we saw . . .

KANT: That clown? (*Others laugh. Kant remains somber.*)

ERASMUS: A clown walked into our world. He gave all of us a gift. (*He begins to laugh and it is contagious. All but Augustine join.*) We can all laugh now. Laugh with the rest of the globe.

HILDEGARD: Laughter is as divine as any good deed we know.

AUGUSTINE: (*A new thought.*) It is the absence of evil. Laughter.

LANGER: Feelings, especially joy, give rise to song, and songs are symbols of life, and those symbols lead to thought. One day at a time.

ERASMUS: (*Impressed.*) Good words, good thoughts.

LANGER: It takes time to know our feelings, and time to feel our thoughts, and often more time to act on them.

GANDHI: Maybe too complicated for me, a simple weaver from India. He seemed to interrupt everything and then, like the wind, left.

HROSTVITHA: Our clown from America did that.

KANT: It is beyond reason.

AQUINAS: Against nature.

AUGUSTINE: And logic.

HILDEGARD: Lacking vision.

HROSTVITHA: An aggravation.

GANDHI: A dodge.

SOCRATES: Again, the question before we were distracted was from our friend Immanuel, who asked whether there can be goodness without God.

AUGUSTINE: Without God, we are all like Adam . . . or Eve—

AQUINAS: I cannot see it any other way.

KANT: But I can. People can learn goodness by reason. (*Pause.*) So how do we reconcile these two views?

AQUINAS: Not possible. They can never meet each other, never converge into one.

HROSTVITHA: With music, such things are possible. I have seen it, known it . . . and experience it each time I see a good play at my convent.

LANGER: The same is true for all the arts. They unite rather than divide.

AUGUSTINE: I dreamed of a city of God filled with sacred awe and set apart from the world.

ERASMUS: That dream began and ended with the feeling that in this needy world, there is work that needs to be done. (*Pause. Augustine is silent.*) We all have work we must do. Each has a field that needs tilling. Aquinas, don't you agree?

(*Aquinas is silent. Pause.*)

KANT: Faith is things unseen but that we long for; reason gives us words for things we have perceived.

SOCRATES: The ideas keep flowing, conversation keeps us going. Now it's time for a walk.

AUGUSTINE: I will go with you. The hot coals that each of you use to torture me are like an angel in disguise.

AQUINAS: Do you really mean that?

AUGUSTINE: We all need to walk in the light and no longer hide behind the dimness of our minds.

HROSTVITHA: That, my Augustine, is very poetic.

ERASMUS: Amazing what joyful impact a clown can have.

HILLEL: I often can sense what is good for all humanity and then examine why I think so. (*To Kant.*) Maybe you, even though you are German, may also laugh again.

KANT: Why pick on me? Augustine didn't laugh either.

AUGUSTINE: Next time, next time, I will. If for no other reason than to laugh at our own folly.

HILLEL: His sorrows are his own. His awakening is also his own.

GANDHI: I told you, sooner or later, we are all shook up by those Americans. Even you, Immanuel.

KANT: Life is too short, too unreasonable, to laugh away our time. We are not that frivolous.

ERASMUS: Immanuel, my friend, frivolity is the taste of freedom.

KANT: I'll need time to digest that.

ERASMUS: Goodness has visited us today, and laughter has given us a gift of unity.

KANT: You claim that laughter lifts us beyond the old debates, the clash of beliefs, and unites us?

ERASMUS: As I stand here, I declare that can we move beyond all that divides us. Laughter is the ingredient that creates joyful harmony. Aquinas and Augustine agree, don't you? (*They both nod.*)

SOCRATES: We are getting close to knowing the answer—

KANT: Even though it goes against reason, I now see that joy and goodness walk hand in hand.

GANDHI: Because that which you do—

KANT: Is good, should all humanity—

ERASMUS: Do the same.

HROSTVITHA: You, Erasmus, you belong here, among us.

HILDEGARD: When you think, a new world awakens. When you laugh, all creation laughs with you.

SOCRATES: Allow me to suggest that laughter is the incarnation of goodness.

GANDHI: The ultimate elixir of the gods!

AQUINAS: It is ironic isn't it, Erasmus, that after a lifetime of serious thought, devotion, and sacrifice, the reward is laughter?

GANDHI: Hmmm . . . Tea, goodness, laughter . . . and life among the luminaries. (*Slowly, one by one, they exit.*)

SOCRATES: (*Among the last of the group.*) Are you coming? (*Exits.*)

ERASMUS: (*Now by himself. Lights begin to dim. Thunder.*) I'll wait. Wait for the storm to pass. Then the light will shine again. (*Picks up the notes Hillel has left, reclines on the bed. Lights slowly fade to dark.*)

(*Segue to Hildegard von Bingen's "O How Wondrous It Is," such as the version recorded by the St. Stanislav Girls' Choir of the Diocesan Classical Gymnasium, conducted by Helena Fojkar Zupančič.*)

End

www.ingramcontent.com/pod-product-compliance
Lightning Source LLC
Chambersburg PA
CBHW061452170626
46811CB00004B/1482